A BIG BOY NOW

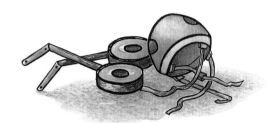

For Wesley, who is a big boy now.
And for Oli, who is catching up.
—E.S.

For Briar, Will, Samuel, and David,
who are big boys now (or will be soon!)
Love, Aunt Megan
—M.L.

A Big Boy Now
Text copyright © 2012 by Eileen Spinelli
Illustrations copyright © 2012 by Megan Lloyd
All rights reserved. Manufactured in China.
No part of this book may be used or reproduced in any manner whatsoever without written
permission except in the case of brief quotations embodied in critical articles and reviews.
For information address HarperCollins Children's Books, a division of HarperCollins Publishers,
10 East 53rd Street, New York, NY 10022.
www.harpercollinschildrens.com
Library of Congress Cataloging-in-Publication Data is available.
ISBN 978-0-06-008673-2 (trade bdg.) — ISBN 978-0-06-008674-9 (lib. bdg.)
Typography by Jeanne L. Hogle
12 13 14 15 16   SCP   10 9 8 7 6 5 4 3 2 1
❖
First Edition

A BIG BOY NOW

by Eileen Spinelli
illustrated by Megan Lloyd

HARPER

An Imprint of HarperCollinsPublishers

I am a big boy now.

In the morning I get dressed.
All by myself.

I make my own bed.

I pour my own cereal,

then I wash my bowl
when I'm done
because
I am a big boy now.

Mom takes me to the playground.
I climb to the very top of the jungle gym.

I fly high on the swing after only one push.

I go down the slide with my hands
in the air.
Mom doesn't have to catch me
because
I am a big boy now.

I help Dad wash his car.
I turn on the hose.
I fill my bucket with soapy water.
I scrub the hubcaps till they are
shiny bright.

Dad is happy to have a helper,
happy that
I am a big boy now.

My friend Jesse comes over to play.
I let Jesse have first turn at my scooter.

When Jesse wins at checkers, I pat him on the back.
I say, "Good job!"

When my baby sister whines for Bananas,
my stuffed monkey,
I let her hold him
because
I am a big boy now.

I can print my name all by myself.

I can color inside the lines.

I can make my own jelly sandwich.

I can stand on one foot for a very long time.

I can stay up a half hour later than before
because
I am a big boy now.

One day I decide to take the training wheels off my bike.

I borrow Dad's screwdriver.
Jesse helps me.
Soon I have a big-boy bike.

No training wheels.
Yippeee!
I ride down the
sidewalk.

I holler to Jesse, "Look at me!"
I laugh out loud.

Then the bike wobbles . . .
wobbles . . .

wobbles.

Uh-oh . . .

uh-oh . . .

I fall smack onto the sidewalk.
I scrape my elbow.
I scrape my knee.
Jesse hurries over. "You're bleeding!" he says.
I start to cry.

I run home to my mom.

She hugs me.
She kisses me.
She washes my elbow and my knee.
She puts a bandage on each boo-boo just like
when I was little.

"I thought I was a big boy," I sniffle.
Mom smiles. "When Dad is hurting, he comes to
me just like you."
"He does?"
"Yep. He comes for a hug and a kiss."
"And a bandage?" I ask.
"Sometimes," she says.

I get my bike.
I set it in the garage.
I think about putting the training wheels back on.

I change my mind.

I don't need training
wheels anymore.

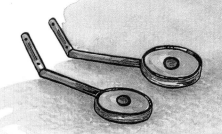

I just practice riding without them.

I can do that.

I am a big boy now.